Sandy
the Dog

by Lynne Benton and Ana Sebastien

W
FRANKLIN WATTS
LONDON•SYDNEY

My name is Sandy.

I live with the Parker family.
I'm teaching them how to
look after me.

I'm teaching Mum how to
tell when I'm hungry.
I pat her knee and look sad.
"Are you hungry, Sandy?"
she says.

I wag my tail.

Then she gives me my food.

I like Mum.

I'm teaching Dad about my toys.

I like chewing rubber bones.

I like chewing rubber balls, too.

He gives me lots of
bones and balls.
I like Dad.

I'm teaching Daisy how to
take me for walks.
I like to sniff good smells.
I like to sniff other dogs, too.

Daisy lets me stop and sniff
when I want to.
I like Daisy.

I'm teaching Tom, too.
I am teaching him
to feed me treats.

I am teaching him
to play football,

and how to read to me.

I like Tom.

My bed is in the kitchen.
Sometimes at night I feel lonely,
so I howl a bit.

13

Tom comes downstairs.

"Poor Sandy," he says.

"Do you want to sleep

on my bed?"

I wag my tail,
and he takes me upstairs.
I like to sleep on his bed.
Tom likes it, too.

Next morning, Mum is cross.

"No, Sandy," she says.

"Your bed is in the kitchen."

"He was lonely," says Tom,

"and so was I."

I wag my tail.

Mum smiles.

"All right, Sandy," she says.

"Thank you for looking after Tom."

The Parker family is learning fast.

I think I will like it here.

Story trail

Start at the beginning of the story trail. Ask your child to retell the story in their own words, pointing to each picture in turn to recall the sequence of events.

Start

Independent Reading

This series is designed to provide an opportunity for your child to read on their own. These notes are written for you to help your child choose a book and to read it independently.

In school, your child's teacher will often be using reading books which have been banded to support the process of learning to read. Use the book band colour your child is reading in school to help you make a good choice. *Sandy the Dog* is a good choice for children reading at Green Band in their classroom to read independently.

The aim of independent reading is to read this book with ease, so that your child enjoys the story and relates it to their own experiences.

About the book

Sandy lives with the Parker family and he is training them how to be the perfect family for him.

Before reading

Help your child to learn how to make good choices by asking: "Why did you choose this book? Why do you think you will enjoy it?" Look at the cover together and ask: "What do you think the story will be about?" Support your child to think of what they already know about the story context. Read the title aloud and ask: "Who do you think will be telling the story in this book?"

Remind your child that they can try to sound out the letters to make a word if they get stuck.

Decide together whether your child will read the story independently or read it aloud to you.

During reading

If reading aloud, support your child if they hesitate or ask for help by telling the word. Remind your child of what they know and what they can do independently.

If reading to themselves, remind your child that they can come and ask for your help if stuck.

After reading

Support comprehension by asking your child to tell you about the story. Use the story trail to encourage your child to retell the story in the right sequence, in their own words.

Help your child think about the messages in the book that go beyond the story and ask: "Do you think the Parker family know they are being trained by Sandy? Why/why not?"

Give your child a chance to respond to the story: "Did you have a favourite part? Do you have a pet? What makes your pet or any pet happy?"

Extending learning

Help your child understand the story structure by using the same story context and adding different elements. "Let's make up a new story about a pet going to live with a new family. Which pet will you choose? What might this pet like to do with their family?"

In the classroom, your child's teacher may be teaching polysyllabic words (words with more than one syllable). There are many in this book that you could look at with your child, for example: chew/ing, learn/ing, look/ing, teach/ing, down/stairs, foot/ball, morn/ing, fam/i/ly, hung/ry, lone/ly.

Franklin Watts
First published in Great Britain in 2020
by The Watts Publishing Group

Series Editors: Jackie Hamley and Melanie Palmer
Series Advisors: Dr Sue Bodman and Glen Franklin
Series Designer: Peter Scoulding

A CIP catalogue record for this book is
available from the British Library.

ISBN 978 1 4451 6867 8 (hbk)
ISBN 978 1 4451 6868 5 (pbk)
ISBN 978 1 4451 6871 5 (library ebook)

Printed in China

Franklin Watts
An imprint of
Hachette Children's Group
Part of The Watts Publishing Group
Carmelite House
50 Victoria Embankment
London EC4Y 0DZ

An Hachette UK Company
www.hachette.co.uk

www.franklinwatts.co.uk

FSC
www.fsc.org
MIX
Paper from
responsible sources
FSC® C104740